Ballet Bruce

By Ryan T. Higgins

DISNEP • HYPERION

Los Angeles   New York

For Cecilia

First Hardcover Edition, May 2022
First Paperback Edition, May 2022
10 9 8 7 6 5 4 3 2 1
FAC-038091-22077
Printed in the United States of America

This book is set in Century OS MT Pro/Monotype
Designed by Tyler Nevins

Library of Congress Cataloging-in-Publication Control Number: 2021940765
Hardcover ISBN 978-1-368-05960-2
Paperback ISBN 978-1-368-08098-9

Reinforced binding on hardcover

Visit www.DisneyBooks.com

The geese want to do ballet today.

But they need help.

Will Bruce help them do ballet?

The geese use sad goose eyes.

"Okay. Fine," says Bruce.

It is hard for Bruce to say no
to sad goose eyes.

Hooray!
It is time for ballet!

Oh, wait!

The geese need
ballet shoes.

Bruce rides into town
to find ballet shoes.

The ride into town
is long.

The ride home is long, too.

Bruce is tired.

But he has the ballet shoes.

Hooray!
It is time for ballet!

Not so fast!

The geese need
fancy dance pants.

The ride into town
is still long.

And the store is out
of fancy dance pants.

Prancing dance pants will have to do.

Bruce is ready to be home.

Bruce is very tired.
  But he has the ballet shoes.
  And he has the prancing dance pants—
    even though the geese wanted
                    fancy dance pants.

Hooray!
It is time for ballet!

Hold on!

The geese need tutus.

Bruce is riding a lot today.

The store has too many tutus.
Bruce does not know which
tutus to buy.

So Bruce buys all the tutus.

This time, the ride home is fast.

It is too fast for Bruce.

Bruce is very, VERY tired.
But he has the ballet shoes.
And he has the prancing dance pants—
  even though the geese wanted
  fancy dance pants.

And he has ALL the tutus.

Hooray?
Is it time for ballet?

Not anymore.

The geese do not
want to do ballet.

Now the geese want Bruce
to take them for a ride.